Other books about
Little White Fish:

Little White Fish
(about colors)

*Little White Fish
Has a Party*

Guido
van
Genechten

Little White Fish Has Many Friends

Clavis
NEW YORK

Little White Fish is a very playful fish.
He loves to **ride** on turtle's **back**.

He **plays tag** with Little Goldfish.
Little White Fish is super-fast!

He **gives** Little Slug **Eskimo kisses,**
until they can't stop laughing.

Little White Fish **plays train** with the Seastar family.
Today, he gets to pull the train.
Toot-toot!

He likes to **play hide-and-seek**
with Little Crab. Little White Fish
looks carefully behind every rock.

'Peek-a-boo!' cries Little crab.
Oops, a bit too early.

Little White Fish loves to **blow bubbles** with octopus. Oh, the bubbles they make are beautiful!

And with Little Shrimp, Little White Fish
dances the cha-cha!

Little White Fish is a very playful fish.
Luckily, he has many friends to play with.
They make him happy every day.

First published in Belgium and Holland by Clavis Uitgeverij, Hasselt – Amsterdam, 2016
Copyright © 2016, Clavis Uitgeverij
English translation from the Dutch by Clavis Publishing Inc. New York
Copyright © 2016 for the English language edition: Clavis Publishing Inc. New York
Visit us on the web at www.clavisbooks.com

Little White Fish Has Many Friends written and illustrated by Guido Van Genechten
Original title: *Klein wit visje heeft veel vriendjes*
Translated from the Dutch by Clavis Publishing

ISBN 978-1-60537-303-4

This book was printed in February 2016 at Publikum d.o.o., Slavka Rodica 6, Belgrade, Serbia

First Edition
10 9 8 7 6 5 4 3 2 1

Clavis Publishing supports the First Amendment and celebrates the right to read